KEVIN CROSSLEY-HOLLAND

SHORT TOO!

A second book of very **SHORT** stories

OXFORD
UNIVERSITY PRESS

OXFORD
UNIVERSITY PRESS

Great Clarendon Street, Oxford OX2 6DP
Oxford University Press is a department of the University of Oxford.
It furthers the University's objective of excellence in research, scholarship,
and education by publishing worldwide in

Oxford New York

Auckland Cape Town Dar es Salaam Hong Kong Karachi
Kuala Lumpur Madrid Melbourne Mexico City Nairobi
New Delhi Shanghai Taipei Toronto

With offices in

Argentina Austria Brazil Chile Czech Republic France Greece
Guatemala Hungary Italy Japan Poland Portugal Singapore
South Korea Switzerland Thailand Turkey Ukraine Vietnam

Oxford is a registered trade mark of Oxford University Press
in the UK and in certain other countries

British Library Cataloguing in Publication Data

Data available

ISBN: 978-0-19-278013-3
5 7 9 10 8 6

Printed in Great Britain
Paper used in the production of this book is a natural,
recyclable product made from wood grown in sustainable forests.
The manufacturing process conforms to the environmental
regulations of the country of origin.

For Chloe and Henry

Kevin Crossley-Holland has won the Carnegie Medal and
the Guardian Children's Fiction Award.
He is also a poet and patron of the Society for Storytelling,
and has been shortlisted to be Children's Laureate.

Contents

Hairy   8
Ship of Death   10
The Radiant Boy   12
The Gift of Gifts   14
Chocolate   16
Cannibals   18
Hide-and-Seek   20
Stone Porridge   22
My Dead Daughter   24
The Hairy Woman   26
The Dream-House   28
Angels   30
A Bagful of Butterflies   32
The Maker of Melons   34
Bluebird and Coyote   36
No Windows and No Doors   38
Black Dog   40
Missed a Bean   42
In Your Dreams   44
Is It True?   46
Dathera Dad   48
Five Plus One   50
Can We Keep It?   52

The Short Life of Barbara the Lamb
  Who Froze to Death   54
The Fox and the Cat   56
Poisoned   58
Head-Louse   60
Ko-Kay-Ke-Ko   62
Sit!   64
Battle Royal   66
That   68
Dance of Death   70
Nic   72
Lookout Lane   74
The Vanishing Hitchhiker   76
Fault Line   78
Mosquitoes   80
Why Everyone Needs to be Able
  to Tell a Story   82
The Double-Tree   84
Nightmare   86
Just One Gulp   88
My Story   90
Between Worlds   92
Storybirds   94

Hairy

It's not so easy to get holiday work round here, so I was pleased when the zoo-lady rang and said they'd got a job for me after all.

I went round at once and the lady led me through a gloomy concrete tunnel—you know, like an underpass—right into the gorilla cage. It was empty, though.

'Poor old Goran,' the lady said. 'He's in our hospital.'

'What's wrong with him?'

'His age! We need a young one, really. Goran just sits up there on that branch all day, holding that swinging rope.'

'Boring,' I said.

'I know. But even a boring gorilla's still a big attraction.' The zoo-lady smiled at me.

'What?'

'We've got this gorilla suit. Will you sit up in that tree so at least the kids have something to look at? Two shifts a day, three hours each. With a lunch-break in between.'

'Sounds good,' I said, grinning. 'Not your usual holiday job.'

'And decent money,' the lady added.

Next morning, I went round and put on my gorilla-suit. I climbed up to the branch and sat on it, and hundreds of visitors were soon pressing their faces against the bars of my cage.

Talk about boring! Before long I was bored out of my mind.

I know what, I thought. And I began to scratch under my armpits, and yelp, and thump my hairy chest.

The kids thought it was great. So then I grabbed the tatty old rope, wrapped myself around it, and swung across my cage.

The kids loved that even more. They laughed and whooped.

In the cage alongside mine, there was a mangy old lion. I could tell he was getting impatient with my antics because he kept pacing round and round, and roaring.

I kept swinging, though. Higher and higher. And when I swung over towards the lion, I pushed off his bars with my feet.

The kids and their parents couldn't get enough of it. They kept laughing and yelling for more.

I swung even higher then, and that's when I missed the bars. I flew right between them, lost my grip on the tatty rope, and dropped into the lion's cage.

Somehow I scrambled up, and I ran towards the visitors, crying, 'Help! Help! I'm not—'

The lion sprang at me from behind. He knocked me flat and lowered his huge head over me.

'Shut up, you idiot!' he growled in a hoarse voice. 'Shut up, or they'll dump us both.'

Ship of Death

They knew they shouldn't have.

They knew what their parents had said about not going down to the beach on their own, what with the galloping spring tide and weirdoes and the blue moon and naturists and worse.

But!

But the beach in the blue hour, it called to them like a wild bird on the wing, hoarse and insistent. And then, looking out of the window of their B & B, they saw the ship.

Without a word, the two of them slipped on their flip-flops. Out they went and away they flew and the damp chill of the early evening embraced them.

They ran across the sandflats, corrugated and sparkling. They crunched across the strip of razor shells, they raced each other down to the water's edge.

The sea was smooth and shiny as silver plate. The skyline was violet. And the skull of the sky was pale, pale blue.

And the ship, the icy ship with her one huge sail, burnt orange? They could almost reach out and touch her. She was drifting, drifting towards them.

Biting cold was coming from the ship. It grabbed them by the ankles, it grasped them round their midriffs, it gripped them round their necks.

Then the helmsman stood up. Dressed in black. He shouted out something, and beckoned to them.

The children could feel their blood freezing in their blue veins. They turned, they sprinted back across the foreshore, the scrunchy razor shells, the corrugated sandflats.

The children's parents gave them a rocket-and-a-half when they got back.

Still, their dad did still tell them a bedtime story, same as usual.

'Yes,' he began, 'quite a coast, this. What with drownings and smugglers and worse.'

'Worse?'

'There's an older story,' he said, and his voice darkened.

'What about?'

'The icy ship.'

Each of them felt a freezing finger at the nape of their necks.

'What's she like?'

Their father shrugged. 'She's got an orange sail and her helmsman is Death. And her cargo? Nothing but spirits.'

The children looked at each other.

'And if you ever see her,' their father went on, 'you mustn't say a word about her. Not to anyone at all. For a year and a day.'

The two children said nothing.

'Otherwise Death will come back for you. He'll come close in, so close you can almost touch the icy gunwales, and you'll have to go aboard.'

'Is that true?'

'Look at you,' said their father, smiling. 'Both of you. What's wrong with you? White and blue. As if you've seen your own ghosts.'

The Radiant Boy

It was last year, and I was ten.

I was in the park, skateboarding, and it was one of those grey, lumpy November afternoons. I'd just dropped in for the first time. That's not such a big deal, I know, but it felt like it was. I was really pleased with myself. Alight, almost.

Well, I was still skating round when I saw my own shadow—me on my board—cruising along just in front of me.

On a grey afternoon. A lumpy afternoon. When there wasn't a shadow in the whole park.

I stared at the shadow, and then I turned round to see what was shining on me.

It was a boy, made of light. He was, well … radiant. Shining bright.

What did he look like? What was he wearing?

I don't know. I mean, I didn't notice anything like that.

What about his board, then? Was that lit up too?

I don't know. I think so.

This boy shot past me without looking back. He rolled right across the park to the far ramp. That's where he put his heel down and stopped.

But then he skated right past the grind bar. Sort of right through it.

What then?

He wasn't there. He was gone.

Me, I was still riding through the gloom.

So is he still ahead, still waiting for me? Is he waiting in the gloom for me to ollie or kick-flip for the first time, and light myself up again?

The Gift of Gifts

'This terrible plague,' said the Mongol horseman, 'it's like a hurricane. Whoever's still strong enough must gallop away from it, and whoever is not must lie low, and hope.'

One of those too weak to ride away from the plague was a young man called Tarvaa. Before long, Tarvaa sent his spirit ahead of his poor body, and it went down to the cold home of the dead in the Underworld.

When the Khan of the Underworld saw the young man, he asked him, 'Why have you left your body? It's still alive.'

'I chose not to wait until you called me,' Tarvaa replied. 'I just came.'

The Khan was moved by Tarvaa's accepting spirit. 'It's not your time yet,' he told him. 'You must go back. But you may take whatever you like with you.'

The young man looked around him, and he saw each and every earthly joy. Friendship, dance, hope, children; he heard music and laughter, he smelt rain and scented flowers, he tasted the fruits of the earth…

Tarvaa turned back to the Khan, knowing the gift that can summon up every other delight in the world. 'Will you,' he asked, 'give me the gift of storytelling?'

So the young man returned to his poor, wasted body only to find that heartless crows had already pecked out its eyes. But the young man had no choice, he had to obey the Khan. So his spirit entered his body and his body lived again; blind, yes, but with his inner eye seeing each and every story, and knowing how to tell it.

For as long as he lived, Tarvaa rode around Mongolia, telling tales, telling legends. And those who heard them smiled, because they knew more about life and all its joys.

Chocolate

It was a cool idea.

I mean, I was meeting Annie's mum for the first time, and she was going to cook tea for us. So I figured that giving her a box of chocolates would please them both. You know, two birds with one stone.

I'd never gone into the chocolate shop before, and it was quite fancy.

'Not too pricey or anything,' I told the man behind the glass counter—he was wearing a straw hat with a scarlet ribbon round it. 'I've only got three quid and it's for my girlfriend's mum.'

'Nice work,' the man said. 'What's she like, then?'

'I haven't met her yet. Actually, my girlfriend says she's a bit of a truffle.' I grinned. 'She's got three chins.'

'Really?' the chocolate-man replied.

'Yes, and she says her dad's a smoothie.'

'Right,' said the man. 'Just a mouthful, then. A taster.'

As soon as I'd shaken hands with Annie's mum, I gave her the little box of chocolates, done up with a ribbon.

'Oh!' squeaked Annie. 'You're so sweet. I hope you picked my favourites.'

Annie's mum pushed the box into her chins. 'They're not

yours,' she said. 'Anyhow, tea's ready. Sit yourselves down.'

When I met Annie's dad, I went hot and cold and soft-centred. I jammed my hands together, and tried to figure out what to do.

'What is it, dear?' asked Annie's mum. 'Are you praying?'

'Yes,' I replied, quick as a snickersnack. 'Yes, we always pray, we say grace before supper.'

'You never told me you were so religious,' Annie said.

'And you,' I whispered in a hoarse voice as soon as her mum and dad had gone out into the kitchen, 'you never told me your dad's got a chocolate shop.'

Cannibals

Lena's old grandparents were upset when they were separated from their granddaughter by the war.

Each week, they sent her and her young family food parcels from America. And even after Grandma died, Grandpa went on sending parcels regular as clockwork. Spam, powdered eggs, sugar, chocolate, and even a pair of outsize shoes for Lena's outsize husband.

Lena couldn't have been more grateful. My two boys are growing so fast, she thought. However much I give them, it's never enough.

When one parcel arrived, it contained a big tin of pale grey powder without a label on it, and Lena wasn't quite sure what it was.

'I'll add it to the broth,' she told her husband.

'Good idea,' he said. 'It will give it some body.'

Within a couple of weeks, Lena's young family had finished off the whole tin, and a few days later she received a letter from her old grandfather.

'Dearest Lena,' he began. 'Did I tell you the unlabelled tin contains Grandma's ashes? Her last wish was to go home. Please can you sprinkle them around the garden she loved so much?'

Hide-and-Seek

Now I know, she thought. Now I know what people mean when they say their hearts are bursting with happiness. I've never felt like this.

More than my wedding dress and this feast, these honey-candles, this grand castle, more even than the talk, the laughter and tears, it's how my man and all my family, all my friends, how they're all here under one roof.

She could hardly bear the wedding feast to come to an end. One more song, she sang. One more dance, she danced. One more tear, she wept. One more kiss …

Then she had an idea.

'I know it's silly, but we'll never all be in one place again. Not like this. Let's play Hide-and-Seek, all my family, all my friends. Let's be children again.'

'Hide-and-Seek!' everyone cried. 'Hide-and-Seek. You hide first.'

Away she went, away from her young husband, out of the echoing hall, carrying one honey-candle. She long-legged it up the wide, creaking staircase. She ran from room to room, she climbed from floor to floor.

At the top of the castle, she found a room with a rough-hewn oak chest in it. The size of a coffin. The top and sides were thick as thick, and it was filled with fleece as soft as down.

She smiled and stepped into the chest. She blew out her candle. She lowered the lid.

At once the lock sprang.

'Ninety-eight, ninety-nine, one hundred ... Ready or not, we're coming!'

Her young husband and all the seekers hurried from room to room, each of them carrying a honey-candle. They long-legged it up the wide, creaking staircase and ran from room to room and climbed from floor to floor.

'Where are you?' they called. 'Not here. No! Where is she?'

She couldn't hear them, though. And her young husband and her family and friends, they couldn't hear her. Not when she called out, when she screamed, not when she banged at the inside of the chest, cocooned as she was inside the stifling fleece.

'Where are you?' they cried. 'Come out now. We can't find you.'

They couldn't find her, no. But she was found, though. Two hundred years later. Inside her wedding-dress, her skull and bones.

Stone Porridge

The young woman rapped at the door of the old man's shack. 'I'm lost,' she said in a husky voice. 'I've been walking through the bush for seven days.'

'On your own?' asked the old man.

'I'm almost out of water, and I haven't eaten for seven days.'

'Neither have I,' said the mean old man. 'Believe me, there's nothing to eat here.'

'In fact,' the young woman told him, 'I'm so hungry I'm not hungry, if you know what I mean. I could do with some soup, though.'

The old man pursed his lips. 'So could I,' he said. 'Believe me.'

'Oh!' the young woman croaked. 'I see you've got that big stone.'

The old man stared at his doorstop.

'We could use that.'

'Use it?'

'To make porridge. Nothing better. I'll show you.'

Then the young woman picked up the dusty stone and dashed some water from the rain-barrel over it.

'Watch it,' the old man warned her. 'Not too much.'

'Well, are you asking me in?' said the young woman. Then she walked over to the hearth and dropped the stone into the cooking-pot hanging over it.

'More water,' she told him. 'That's all I need. You can't make porridge without water.'

The old man grumbled a bit and brought the young woman a jug full of water. Then he watched her carefully as she stirred the pot and tasted the water.

'Pity there's no salt,' she sighed.

'Here,' said the old man, and he gave her a pinch of salt. Then he tapped his head. 'Seven days,' he said. 'The sun's touched you, that's what.'

The young woman tasted the water again. 'Not bad,' she said in her husky voice. 'Not bad at all. Back home, it tastes even better if we add a handful of barley.'

'I've only got oats,' said the old man.

'They'll do, then,' the young woman told him. 'Just half-a-handful.'

Then the old man found himself a second spoon. So there they stood, one on either side of the cooking-pot, and they began to eat.

'Stone porridge,' marvelled the old man. 'To think I've lived so long and never known about it.'

'Nothing better,' the young woman said.

My Dead Daughter

Posy had only gone down to the supermarket for a couple of things—milk and sugar. But there was quite a queue at the Ten Items or Less checkout counter, so she joined one of the other lines instead.

Once the woman in front of her had stacked all her purchases on to the moving belt, she turned round to face Posy.

'Oh! Dear heaven!' she exclaimed. 'Daisy! My dead daughter. You've come back to life again.'

'No, I'm not,' said Posy.

'Daisy! You are! You are, aren't you?'

'No,' said Posy. 'I'm Posy. Posy Reynolds.'

'And you're fourteen.'

'Ye-es,' said Posy.

'Well! You gave me a shock, you did,' the woman said. 'Peas in a pod. I'm quite breathless.' The woman put her right hand over her heart. 'I'll tell you what. When I'm through here, will you call out, "Bye, Mum?"'

'Weird,' said Posy.

'Will you, sweetheart?' the woman asked. 'That'll do my poor old heart good, it will.'

As soon as the woman had bagged her purchases, she had

24

a quick word with the checkout assistant and then called out, 'Bye, sweetheart.'

'Bye, Mum,' said Posy, shaking her head.

Then the checkout assistant scanned Posy's purchases—the milk and the sugar.

'£119.20,' she said.

'What?' exclaimed Posy, laughing. 'For milk and sugar?'

'And all your mum's purchases.'

Posy drew in her breath. 'She's not my mum.'

'She is and all. I heard you.'

'No.'

'"Bye, Mum!" That's what you said. She told me you were going to pay.'

The Hairy Woman

This actually happened to someone I know. I know her well. My own daughter! That's why I'm sure it's true.

Coral—that's her—she was down at the supermarket for the weekly shop. Friday, five-ish. It's always crowded, she says, but she works until half-past-four so she can't go before that.

Coral was in the car park. She'd just loaded all the plastic bags into the boot when a big woman lurched up to her. You know, a bit of a lump. Specs. Powerful eyebrows. She was wearing a long dark skirt.

'Give me a lift, love?' the woman asked. 'Just down to the bus stop. I've only got this one bag but it's that heavy.'

'Hop in,' said my daughter. 'You can put your bag on the back seat.'

But halfway down the road, Coral saw how big and blunt and rough the woman's fingertips were. And then she looked down. Below her dark skirt and above her boots, her passenger had hairy, muscular legs, and a shining knife was taped to the right one.

Cor! My Coral, she didn't half think fast. She braked. She braked hard. 'Hang on!' she exclaimed. 'There's my dad! That policeman.'

Her passenger didn't hang around. He swung the door open and scrambled out. He scrambled out so fast he forgot his canvas bag.

You know what was in it. A hammer, yes. And a wicked axe. And a sharp-toothed saw.

The Dream-House

'January second,' said Millie's father. 'So we've got nine months to find a new house.'

Almost as soon as Millie knew that she and her parents had to move because of her father's new job, she began to dream.

'The house of my dreams,' she told her mother. 'I keep seeing it. It's not that posh but it's got an old walnut tree and a little frog-pool and the stairs sort-of twist round to the left as you go up, and there are three bedrooms … '

'Three!' exclaimed her mother.

'In your dreams!' said Millie's father.

' … but one's as small as a matchbox.'

Night after night, Millie visited her dream-house, until she knew it outside in and inside out. Each cupboard and corner, each paving-stone and grassblade.

The first time Millie and her parents looked at houses, the ones they liked were all too expensive. But on their second expedition, they went to see a small house in a little village.

'I know it's a very good price,' said Millie's mother, 'but I can't see myself living in the country. I really can't.'

The moment she saw the house with the FOR SALE sign outside it, Millie exclaimed, 'This is it! My dream-house.'

Millie's mother clicked her tongue. 'You and your dreams,' she said.

'It is! I'll prove it.'

When the woman who owned the house opened the door and saw Millie and her parents on the porch, she went quite white.

'I know it seems rather strange,' Millie told her, 'but can I show my mum and dad round?'

The owner shook her head. 'Help yourself,' she said.

So that's what Millie did. She showed them the stairs that sort-of twisted round to the left and the three bedrooms, one as small as a matchbox, and everything else.

But when she came to a green baize door between the kitchen and the little garden, Millie was puzzled, 'I haven't seen that before,' she said.

The owner smiled. 'How do you mean, dear?'

'I haven't.'

'It's for insulation,' the owner told her. 'My husband and I only put it in a couple of weeks ago.'

When Millie's parents went to see the estate agent, they asked him why the house was selling at such an attractive price.

The agent smiled and peered at Millie over the top of his spectacles. 'Well,' he said. 'It's cock-and-bull, really.'

'What do you mean?' asked Millie's mother.

'The owner says the house is haunted. She's seen the ghost wandering from room to room almost every night for the last nine months.'

Millie's mother pursed her lips and looked at her husband.

'But you needn't worry. The owner says it's your daughter,' the agent went on. 'Millie is the ghost!'

Angels

True, he was free.

Free to get up when he wanted, eat and drink when he wanted, go to bed when he wanted.

But he had no dear ones. He was only. And lonely, too, his neighbours said.

His only regret was he never had any children.

Little devils, said one neighbour.

You know, he told them. Just a solo. Or a duet.

Twins, you mean.

Yes. Or a trio.

His one friend was his old guitar. He used to play to himself, and warble, and sometimes he went on half the night. And just once, playing away the dark, he knew he was playing in a way he'd never done before. Playing like an angel. He laughed and he wept.

He used to play with his eyes closed, he did. But when he opened them, he saw a light shining outside his window. Bright strips between the shutter's wooden boards.

He got up. He unlatched the door to see who was there.

Three angels. Three newborn babies, each of them no more than one foot tall.

They'd heard the music and come down from above.

And, side by side, up on the sill, in their own light they were dancing.

A Bagful of Butterflies

The Maker stared at his world.

Everything I've made is so beautiful, he thought.

Children, yes. Children especially.

I think I'll save the most lovely colours in my world to brighten their grey days.

So the Maker opened his bag and began to put colours into it. A spot of sunlight. Orange petals, pink petals. A window of blue plucked from between the rolling clouds. The gleam of a girl's hair so black that it was green.

Yes, thought the Maker. And I'll add some snatches of song to my bag as well.

When the children untied the Maker's bag, out fluttered thousands and thousands of butterflies. Silver-spotted, green hairstreak and chalkhill blue, orange-tip and clouded yellow, peacock and painted lady, their wings were every colour that there is. And then the butterflies began to warble and twitter and chirp—to sing!

'Just listen to them,' said the Maker.

But at once a storm of birds flew in from the north and south and east and west. They swirled around the Maker and many of them sat on his shoulders and whistled in his ears.

'You've given them our songs. You've given them away!'

'You promised we'd each have a song of our own.'

'You've broken your word.'

The Maker sighed. 'It's true,' he said. 'I should never have done so.'

So he took their songs back from all the butterflies. That's why they're silent.

'Even so,' the Maker told the children. 'Just look at them.'

The Maker of Melons

How many water-melons were heaped on that rickety ox-cart? Hundreds and hundreds. Maybe a thousand.

An old man toddled up to the cart's drivers who were sitting in its shadow, each devouring one of the ripe fruit. 'Can you spare me one?' he asked.

'Push off!' said the first driver.

The second driver took another huge mouthful out of his melon. He sucked and slurped, then he spat out a dozen pips at the old man's feet.

'It's so hot,' said the old man. 'The dust's in my throat.'

'They're not ours to give,' said the second driver. 'We've been hired by the farmer to take them to market.'

'You wouldn't give one to your dying grandmother,' said the old man.

'Move on, you old fungus!' said the first driver.

'All right,' said the old man. 'If you won't give me a melon, I'll have to grow one for myself.'

'You do that,' said the first driver.

Then the old man bent down and picked up a few of the pips the second driver had spat out. Next, he drew a square on the ground with his stick, scratched the dusty earth, and dropped the pips into it.

One driver tapped his forehead; the other raised his eyes.

But the old man didn't see them. Carefully, he sprinkled dust over the pips, just a handful of it, and then he spat on them.

Yellow-green tendrils sprouting from the ground; vines twisting and surging; pale blossom blooming, then withering; firm fruit budding, then swelling, ripening ...

And all this in no more time than it takes to eat a water-melon! The drivers got to their feet and inched forward. A small crowd of people gathered and silently watched the crop of water-melons growing by the roadside.

Now the old man began to harvest his crop. He gave his first melon to the first driver, and the second melon to the second driver. He offered one melon to each child and each woman and each man, until he had picked the whole crop.

'So,' said the old man. 'What generous pips! And how generous the earth is, and the sun!'

'Who is he?' the first driver whispered.

'A magician,' muttered the second.

'Time I was on my way,' said the old man. He stared at the drivers and the crowd, and half-smiled. Then he toddled off down the dusty road.

For some time no one was able to take their eyes off him; and then they stared again at the melon-patch, and finished the tasty fruit he had given them.

'Come on!' said the first driver. 'It'll be dark before we get to market.'

But when the two men turned round, there were no longer a thousand melons piled high on their cart. No, there was not even one.

Bluebird and Coyote

Before Bluebird won her name, her feathers were dim and dun and dismal—and everything else beginning with D.

'Dreary,' barked Coyote. 'Plain dreary. You've got the most dreary feathers in the forest. Even dreary birds taste good, though.'

One day Bluebird flew to a nearby lake, and Coyote followed her. Bluebird looked longingly at the water. It wasn't only turquoise or only indigo, and it wasn't only storm-cloud or ice-blue. No, it was the blue containing every other blue.

Early on the next two mornings, Bluebird bathed in the lake, and sang: 'Blue of blue. Blue of blue. And down in this water, I'm blue too.'

Coyote listened and wanted to jump in. He wanted to eat Bluebird for his breakfast, but he was afraid of the water.

On the fourth morning, Bluebird shed her dreary feathers and came out of the water bare as a baby's bottom. But when she bathed in the lake on the fifth morning, she grew new feathers, and they were blue of blue.

'Look at you!' marvelled Coyote. 'More beautiful than any other bird.'

'Because I bathed in the lake,' said Bluebird. 'And because I sang.'

'I want to be blue,' barked Coyote. 'But I don't like deep water.'

'Be brave,' Bluebird told him. 'Five times—that's all. I'll teach you the song.'

So Coyote was brave, and jumped into the water, howling the song Bluebird had taught him. On the fourth morning he shed all his hair, and on the fifth morning he stepped out of the water blue of blue.

Coyote was so proud. Proud of proud! As he walked along, he kept glancing to the left and right and all around him, hoping the other beasts and birds would see how splendid and blue he was.

Coyote was so proud and pleased that he began to trot and then to run, to run very fast. And as he ran, he looked down to check whether his shadow was as blue as he was.

Because he wasn't looking where he was going, Coyote bumped straight into the stump of a pine tree, and fell over sideways. He rolled over and over on the dusty ground, and all his blue hair turned dusty.

'Dull and dismal,' Bluebird sang. 'Plain dusty.'

So that's why Coyote and all his descendants have been dust-coloured from that day to this.

No Windows and No Doors

Hidden in the heart of the forest, there was a meadow freckled with yellow and mauve wild flowers, fringed with moths with sepia and ashen wings.

And in the middle of this meadow crouched a small building, not much larger than a hut or a caravan. Its walls were limestone blocks, roughly dressed, its roof was slate, and it looked as if it had grown out of the ground. It had no windows and no doors.

Mel and Lucy walked round it. And then round again to make sure.

'So how do you get in?' asked Mel.

'Or out?' added his sister.

'And if you do get in, can you ever get out again?'

'Maybe there's a tunnel,' Lucy suggested.

But there was no tunnel.

'So what's inside it?' asked Mel.

'It isn't an ordinary place and so it won't be anything ordinary,' Lucy said. 'Except creepy-crawlies. They get in everywhere.'

Mel pressed his nose against the rough stone wall, and squinted through one of the gaps between the stone blocks, but he couldn't see a thing.

'Whatever it is,' he said in a dark voice, 'it's something that has to be kept dark.'

'Because you'd be ashamed if anyone knew about it,' his sister suggested.

'Or something that lives in the dark.'

'Like nightmares,' said Lucy. 'Or is it that box? When you open it, everything bad and evil flies out.'

Lucy and Mel backed away a bit. Mel sucked the pith out of a piece of grass, and Lucy picked a flower, bright and shiny as butter.

'Maybe it's full of good things,' Lucy volunteered.

'Like a time capsule, you mean?'

'Sort of. But nothing ordinary, that's what we said. Only best things.'

'Such as?'

'I don't know. Memories. Hopes.'

'You can't store memories,' Mel told her. 'Not unless you're a brain.'

'Maybe nothing, then,' his sister said. 'What about that? Maybe it's a place full of nothing.'

Mel snorted. 'Why would you bother to build a place for nothing …'

Yes, why would you?

So, what's the way in? And what's hidden there?

This story, how is it to end? That's up to you. And down to you.

Black Dog

When Winnie and Kate went hiking, they stayed one night at a windmill. With their gently curving outer walls, their little rooms looked like half-moons, one above the other.

On the fourth floor, Winnie didn't sleep well at all. She dreamed that a black dog glared at her through the salt-stained window panes, and then leaped into the room, and pawed her all over. She screamed. How she screamed. But no one saved her.

When Winnie woke early next morning, in the misty light, she still felt very upset. But there was no sign of the dog. Not a scratch or a bite. Not one paw print. Nothing.

I'm never coming near this place again, she thought. I've never had such a horrible nightmare.

As soon as Winnie had got dressed, she creaked down the circular staircase to Kate's room, but Kate had already gone downstairs.

'I couldn't sleep,' she explained. 'Or rather, I did sleep but I had a horrible nightmare.'

Winnie shook her head. 'You too.'

'Yes, I dreamed a black dog glared at me through my little window, and then it leaped in, and pawed me all over.'

'Are you serious?' asked Winnie.

'Real,' said Kate.

'I mean, it's as if you just stepped into my head. As if you just told me what I was going to tell you.'

'You know what?' said Kate. 'I just told the warden or whatever she's called, and she showed me the grave right beneath our windows.'

'What grave?'

'A huge black dog. Big as a pony. But people heard it barking after it was buried.'

'Are you serious?' asked Winnie.

'"You're not the first." That's what the warden told me. "And you won't be the last."'

Missed a Bean

Terrible. It was an absolutely terrible summer. Arrow-showers; bouncing hail; and worst of all, the levelling north wind.

There wasn't a farmer in the whole district with a decent crop except for the ones who had planted sugar-beet. Beet bottoms are so tough they'd survive Judgement Day.

All the farmers who had planted tops—you know, wheat and barley and rye and that—they were in despair, and none more so than the old man who lost his whole crop of broad beans.

He sat on a tree stump at the edge of his sodden field and buried his head in his hands. I've had enough, he thought. I'll sell up.

Then the old man sensed someone was standing beside him. A little fellow. Blinking and smiling. He had a big nose, his hair was neatly combed, and he was wearing a smart tweed jacket and a skinny red tie.

'Bad?' mumbled the man in a low-pitched voice.

The farmer nodded.

The little fellow stepped straight into the squelch, and bent down beside the nearest row of beans. He mumbled something or other and when he turned round again, his

42

arms were full of healthy broad beans.

The old farmer's eyes opened wide as saucers.

The little fellow smiled a sweet smile and dropped the beans at the old farmer's feet. Then stepped into the squelch again.

A moment later, he came back again with a second armful of beans.

The old farmer stood up. He followed the little fellow into the field and watched as he mumbled and laid his hand on one sodden black stalk after another and then cropped its beans.

'I've never seen anything like it,' the old man exclaimed. 'Nothing. How can I repay you?'

The little fellow smiled and shook his head.

'Tell me your name, then.'

The little fellow tried to wipe some mud off his jacket but only managed to make it more muddy. He drew himself up to his full height, such as it was.

'Mr Bean,' he mumbled.

In Your Dreams

Summer, morning, field, detector, corner, sides, silence, nothing. Autumn, afternoon, field, same, detector, mounds, hollows, silence, nothing. Winter, firelight, yawn, bed, dream, field, same, detector, rings, dozens. Spring, midnight, yawn, bed, dream, again, field, same, middle, detector, rings, hundreds. Breakfast, field, middle, detector, buzz, dig, rings, thousands, silver, gold.

Is It True?

The woman carefully cupped her right hand in her left hand. Then she shuffled down the icy street, holding her hands out in front of her.

'Like she's carrying a precious gift,' said one neighbour, shivering. 'Poor soul.'

'Like she's begging,' said another.

The woman's third neighbour pointed to her forehead. Then she wrapped her arms around herself and clicked her tongue. It sounded as if she were striking a match.

Before long, a couple of curious young children followed the woman down the frozen street. Then several of their friends crossed the road, wondering what they were missing.

'She's carrying something precious,' one girl told them.

'Pff!' said a boy. His breath condensed in front of him.

'That spark!' exclaimed the youngest. 'I saw it.'

The woman turned round to face the children, and stopped.

'There!' said the youngest. 'I told you.'

'Not,' said the boy. He began to shiver.

'She's right!' said another girl. 'Tongues. Look!'

The woman nodded and smiled, and blew gently on her

46

cupped hands. Then she got down on her haunches and the children crowded round her.

In a little while, they were all kneeling in a circle on the frosty pavement. They held out their cold hands to the bowlful of orange flames. Their eyes flickered.

Dathera Dad

The kitchen was a magic box, full of light and dancing shadows. Shafts of winter sunlight lanced the range, the dresser, and the pail of milk, and the hawthorn tree shivered outside the window.

The farmer's wife hummed as she put the large saucepan of water on the range, and mixed the ingredients—flour and eggs and breadcrumbs, sugar, salt, suet, then nutmeg, cinnamon and other spices.

'And now the brandy,' she said, pouring a generous dollop into the mixture, and then a second dollop for good measure.

The farmer's wife put the mixture into a white bowl and covered it with muslin tied round the rim. Then she lowered it into the steaming water.

As soon as the pudding felt the heat of the water, it jumped out of the saucepan. It rolled in its bowl over the sunlit range and fell on to the floor, and the white bowl cracked. It wheeled across the floor towards the farmer's wife.

At that moment, there was a loud knock and Tom the tramp put his head round the back door.

'Morning, missus,' he said. 'Can you spare a pair of shoes?'

'I can't, Tom,' said the farmer's wife.

'Christmas, missus.'

'Here! You can have this pudding, then,' said the farmer's wife, bending down and picking up the pudding in the cracked white bowl. 'Christmas pudding!'

'Thanks, missus,' said Tom, and he put the pudding in his sack, and slung it over his back.

But Tom was only a few yards down the frosty road when he felt something lumping and jumping so he stopped and opened his sack.

The pudding rolled on to the road. The white bowl broke into pieces, and the pudding burst open ... And out stepped a little fairy child who took one look at Tom the tramp and cried, 'Take me home to my dathera dad! Take me home to my dathera dad!'

Five Plus One

Billy wasn't best at spelling. And he wasn't best at maths. He wasn't best at anything.

But one afternoon he was grinning from ear to ear when his mother collected him from school.

As soon as he'd dumped his school bag on the kitchen table, he got a piece of scrap paper out of a kitchen drawer and a pencil out of the chipped mug.

I HAV MADE SIX MISSTAKES IM
THIS CENTENSE.

That's what Billy wrote.

'Can you find them, Mum?'

Billy's mother frowned.

'Jo told me how,' said Billy. 'But I've changed it.'

Billy's mother shook her head. She patiently crossed out the words Billy had spelt wrongly. 'HAV should be *have* and MISSTAKES should be *mistakes* and IM should be *in*. That's three. And look, Billy, there are two mistakes in the last word. CENTENSE should be *sentence*. So there are five mistakes, not six.'

His mother looked at Billy. 'Why are you grinning like that?' she asked, and she couldn't help smiling herself.

'You've missed one,' Billy told her.

'No,' said Billy's mother, frowning. 'No, I haven't.'
'Number Six is saying there are six mistakes when there's
only five.'

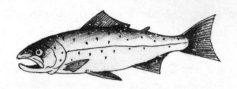

Can We Keep It?

As soon as we got home from the zoo, Jake and his friend Ned, and Plum and her friend Pimpernel—I mean, would you give your daughter a name like that?—they all went upstairs.

'Supper in twenty minutes,' I called after them.

'No hurry, Mum,' said Jake.

No hurry? Normally, they're ravenous.

When I went upstairs myself, all four children were in the bathroom. I listened outside. Splashing. Low voices. Giggling.

'What on earth are you four up to?' I demanded as I swung open the door.

Then I saw. It! And when it saw me, it sort of croaked—croaked and chattered—and rocked from side to side.

'Isn't it sweet?' said Plum.

'Sweet?'

'It's not fully grown yet,' Pimpernel explained.

'Was this you, Jake?'

'Yes, Mum.'

'And me,' said Ned. 'We doubled back!'

'Can we keep it?'

'Don't be ridiculous! I'm going straight downstairs to

phone the zoo.'

I could have guessed. The zoo's switchboard was already on automatic. So it did have to stay for the night.

First it stuffed itself on every fishfinger in the house, and the odd piece of dried-out smoked mackerel at the back of the fridge. Then it made itself comfortable in the bath.

Next morning, all the lines to the zoo were engaged. It took me a long time to get through.

'There's a penguin here,' I began. 'Yes, I *am* being serious.'

'Right,' said a voice at the other end. 'Is that all, then?'

'Isn't that enough?'

'It certainly is, ma'am,' said the voice. 'One elephant . . . one tiger . . . You practical jokers!'

'No! Let me explain.'

Click. The line went dead.

The Short Life of Barbara the Lamb Who Froze to Death

B aa!
Brr!
Ahh!

The Fox and the Cat

'Good day, old friend,' said the cat. 'How are you? How are you getting on in these tough times?'

The arrogant fox inspected the cat from head to tail.

'Tough times?' he drawled. 'You whisker-licker! You mouse-pouncer! A creature with skills like mine doesn't have tough times.'

'I've only got one skill,' the cat said modestly.

'Only one,' scoffed the fox.

'I can climb trees.'

'Is that all?' said the fox. 'I'm master of more than one hundred skills and what's more, I've got a sack full of tricks. I'll teach you how to chase down a rabbit, and how to get into a hen coop. You come with me and I'll teach you how to give a pack of hounds the slip.'

While they were talking, a hunter came through the wood with four hounds. The cat leaped nimbly into a tree, and sat at the top of it where she was completely hidden by branches and leaves.

'Untie your sack, Mr Fox, untie your sack!' the cat called down to him, but the four hounds had already sunk their teeth into him.

'For all your skills and tricks, you're done for,' the cat called out. 'One skill's quite sufficient if it's the right one.'

Poisoned

Megan had spent more than two days in the kitchen cooking for her dinner party. Three, almost.

The last thing she put out on the dining table was the baked salmon. An entire salmon. Lying on its bed of parsley, flanked by lemon slices, it looked so pink and delicate, so plentiful, so royal.

When she checked the table for one last time, Megan realized she'd forgotten the twisted cheese fingers, so she went back to the kitchen to get them. But when she returned to the dining-room, she saw her young cat, Princess, had jumped up on to the table and was helping herself to the salmon.

'No!' she yelled, and she scooped up Princess and threw her out of the garden door.

At that moment, the front doorbell rang, and Megan quickly stuffed a piece of lemon into the salmon where Princess had been nibbling it, and then she covered it with a large sprig of parsley.

'What a spread!' exclaimed Megan's guests. 'Just look at that salmon! Fit for . . . a queen!'

After everyone had eaten their fill, one of Megan's guests opened the back door to go out for a smoke.

On the doorstep lay Princess. She was dead. Stone dead.

Just a poor furry rag without a purr in her.

Megan knew what she had to do. She knew she had no choice. Feeling rather breathless, she told her guests how Princess had jumped up on the table before the party began, and helped herself to the salmon.

'Food poisoning,' she said. 'It must be.'

'I'm going straight down to the Outpatients,' one of the guests said.

'Me too.'

'What about Evan and Alice?' said Megan. 'They've already gone home. I'd better ring them.'

So Megan and all her guests hurried down to the Cottage Hospital to have their stomachs pumped.

Early next morning, Megan's neighbour rang the doorbell, and clutched Megan's arm. 'I can't tell you how sorry I am,' she began. 'Oh, Megan! I was backing the car out of the garage and ran straight over Princess.'

Megan put one hand over her mouth and the other over her stomach.

'I knew you were having that big dinner party,' her neighbour said, 'so I just crept round the back, and laid her out on the doorstep.'

Head-Louse

The strange thing was the boy couldn't hear it and couldn't feel it. But that didn't stop him thinking about it. He knew it was there and he kept thinking how it might be burrowing right into his brains.

But at last the boy caught the head-louse and looked at it wiggling on the palm of his left hand.

'Don't hurt me,' pleaded the louse. 'I haven't hurt you, have I?'

'You've done as much harm as you can,' said the boy.

The head-louse wiggled some more. 'I've got no choice.'

'So,' said the boy, 'give me one good reason why I shouldn't squash you.'

'You have a choice,' the louse replied.

Ko-Kay-Ke-Ko

My old ministers. They're airheads. Chicken-brains! The whole lot of them. So I was quite relieved when this young blade came to court.

Not for long, though. He's so full of himself, and thinks he knows everything. He talks all day, and he'd talk all night if I let him.

It wasn't long before I grew so fed up with his endless words and wit that I decided to teach him a lesson.

I called in all my ministers. 'Tomorrow morning,' I told them, 'we'll go to the lotus-pond, and I want each of you to bring an egg in your pocket. Please, chicken-brains, be careful not to break them.'

'Cluck, cluck!' they all agreed. 'Cluck!'

'And when I give the order, you're to jump into the water, clucking like chickens. Then hold up your eggs. Now whatever you do, don't tell our young friend.'

Early next morning, my old ministers and I strolled over to the lotus-pond, and Know-All came with us. We all admired the white lotus flowers, and then I ordered my ministers to jump into the pond.

'I'm serious,' I told them. 'In you go! Jump in one by one, and lay an egg.'

In they jumped. The whole pond was full of squawking, flapping ministers. And then each of them held up his egg.

'You too,' I told Know-All. 'In you go, and lay an egg. If you don't, I'll dismiss you.'

Know-All gave me a keen look. Then he dived into the pond, and came up crowing, 'Ko-kay-ke-ko! Ko-kay-ke-ko!'

'Where is it?' I called out. 'Your egg.'

'Sir,' said Know-All, 'I don't lay eggs. Let all your chicken-brains lay you eggs! No, I'm a golden cockerel, and I'll greet the sun as it rises on your shining days.'

Sit!

The three young men arrived for their interviews at the same time.

Three applicants for one job, and a first job at that. They all felt anxious.

'Thirteenth floor,' the receptionist told them. 'The lift's over there.'

When the men entered the interview room, they saw it was completely bare—no tables, no chairs—and there was no one to interview them.

Then a big, unsmiling, leathery woman walked in, followed by her dog.

She inspected the three applicants and then reached for her pocket.

'All right,' she said. 'Sit!'

The anxious young men looked at each other. They looked around the room.

'I said sit!' the woman said again, much more firmly.

At once all three young men dropped to the floor, and sat upright and cross-legged.

The woman pulled out her handkerchief, and looked at them, grinning.

'No!' she said. 'I meant the dog.'

Battle Royal

From above, you can see the whole battlefield at one glance.

I guess that's why generals (and kings, too) used to command their troops from hilltops.

But down here at ground-level, you're right in the thick of it. You can hear the sounds of battle—the scraping and shuffling, the breathing silences, and then the sudden strike. You can smell it. You can almost taste it.

However often I fight, I never tire of it. And there's nothing I like better than the openings, the first shots. As often as not, cautious footsoldiers inching forward step by step. The gap between the two armies narrowing.

Here and there a skirmish, a flurry-and-scurry. One man bites the dust. Cat-and-mouse stuff.

Now a horseman springs up—one of ours, or one of theirs. Forwards, sideways, almost dancing on the spot. His hooves striking sparks from the flinty battlefield.

Has there ever been a battle without crooked men claiming that God is fighting on their side? Slanty-eyed bishops, they couldn't walk and talk straight even if they wanted to!

And now my wife is on the move. Truth is, she is much more of a leader than I am, and everyone knows it. All I do is shelter behind my white guards, or watch from the castle shadows, while she cuts across the lines, and spearheads our attack.

All my men are inspired by her; all my opponents are extremely wary of her.

'Check!' says a voice.

The black commander.

I'll step forward. No . . . Sideways, then. I feel so very old, so helpless.

'Mate!' he says.

He stretches, and stands up from the board, and grins.

That

My old mother used to live near a little river. Well, it was less than a river but more than a stream. Each winter it broke its banks and the fields all round looked like silver sheets.

Not far from her cottage was the bridge. The THAT bridge. Everyone knew about the THAT. Some nights you could hear it howling or moaning, so most people wouldn't go near the place after dark. I did, though. Heck! The pub was on the other side and the only other bridge was a good half-mile downstream.

One winter evening, I stopped on the bridge to look at all the shining fields.

Suddenly the THAT came charging up behind me, and it was howling. It was dark and flapping, flapping, and it tried to spike me.

I got out of the way! Fast! So fast I took a header right over the bridge into the January water. And by the time I'd hauled myself out of the water, the THAT had disappeared.

Well, I hurried straight back home and had a hot bath. Next night, though, I did get over to the pub.

'Up on the bridge,' I told my mates. 'Dark and flapping.'

'You're right,' said a voice down at the far end of the

counter. 'I saw him too.'

All my mates turned round.

'Standing on the bridge,' said this bloke. 'The THAT! So I levelled this umbrella. Ha! This spike. That did for him. Where were you, then?'

Dance of Death

'Dance with me at the disco?'
Brian sounded like a lion but he felt like a mouse. And he knew he was starting to blush.

'Yeah!' said Rachel.

'Really?'

'I just said so.'

But Brian had to miss the disco. That Friday, his grandfather was suddenly taken ill, so as soon as school was out his mother drove up north to see him, and Brian went with her.

'Where is he?' Rachel shouted.

'What?' yelled her friends.

'Brian!'

'He never shows up!'

'I thought he was with Carmen.'

Now Brian wasn't there, Rachel really wished he were . . . She wished she could dance with him.

Right at the end of the disco, when the speakers were blasting and the lights flashing, someone grabbed Rachel from behind. He put both his strong hands round her waist and whirled her round and round, round and right down to the end of the gym.

Rachel squealed. Then she screamed. Nothing, not even

the dipper at the fair, had ever felt as wild as this.

Round and round. Rachel spun. She whirled. She thought she was going to die.

When the music stopped and the hands let go of her waist, Rachel turned round to see who owned them.

'Brian!' she gasped.

'The last dance,' panted Brian.

Then he kissed her and walked away. Out of the bright gym.

Rachel shook her head. It was still spinning! 'Weird!' she said. Then she ran back to her friends. 'Did you see him?' she yelled.

'Who?'

'Brian!'

'As if,' her friends shouted.

Just a few minutes later, Rachel's father picked her up and, at home, her mother was waiting up. She knew something must be wrong when they asked her to sit down between them.

'It's very bad news,' her mother told her. 'You know, darling. Your friend, Brian.'

'A car crash,' said her father. 'Him and his mother.'

'That's impossible,' Rachel heard herself say.

'I'm afraid so,' said her father. 'On the motorway. It was on TV.'

Nic

Nic paid for the trainers with a fifty-pound note.

The store manager in the shopping centre held the note up to the light and then strode round the counter and grabbed Nic by the collar.

'Got you!' he growled. 'This note's forged!'

'Let me go,' protested Nic, and he tried to wrestle free.

'Not bloody likely,' the manager said. 'I'm calling the police.'

In the interview room, Nic sat facing two constables. Five pinkish fifties lay on the table between them.

'Forged,' said one constable. 'The whole lot.'

'So what's the scoop, Nic?' the other one asked. 'The tape's running.'

'I went down to the shopping centre,' Nic began, 'and this guy, he sneezed. Then he fished in his denims, like, and something dropped out. I picked it up, this roll of bank notes. Big as a toilet roll.'

'Very pictorial,' one constable said.

'Big as that, and he didn't notice?' the other asked.

'No. So I ran after him and gave them back and he . . .' Nic waved at the fifties in front of him, ' . . . he peeled these ones off.'

'Two hundred and fifty quid!'

'You expect us to believe that?'

'Yes,' insisted Nic. 'I didn't know they were forged. I didn't.'

'In your own words, Nic,' one policeman said.

'The tape's running,' said the other.

'And then in a low voice, this guy said, like, "Thanks, mate. Now, take my advice! Scarper! Keep away from here this afternoon." '

'Keep away from here this afternoon,' repeated the constable.

'Yes.'

'All right, Nic,' the other policeman said, fingering one of the fifties. 'We're going to get real. You're going to tell us who your mate is and what he looks like and why he gave you these and everything else . . . Everything.'

At that moment, the police station was rocked by the most enormous blast. A bomb had exploded in the shopping centre. Hundreds of people were injured and seven poor Saturday shoppers were blown to kingdom come.

Lookout Lane

He felt scared, did Jack, the moment he wheeled round into gloomy Lookout Lane. He had been down it before, but only in his parents' car. He gripped the handlebars, half-stood up and pushed his feet against the pedals.

When he looked down, Jack could see the lane's black blisters in the dying light, its bald patches, and the way in which coarse, ragged plants—the ones that never take no for an answer—had burst through its spine.

Jack glanced to left and right. On one side was the drainage ditch, choked and oozing; on the other, overhanging bushes, thick, clutching hiding-places. It's like a canyon, he thought. There's no escape.

Then Jack stood right up on his pedals. He yelled. He rang his bell. He rang it and rang it as if he could ring danger away.

Faster he rode, did Jack. And the lane grew rougher and darker.

I wish I'd stayed on the main road, he thought. Then he saw a big sign:

CATS EYES HAVE BEEN REMOVED

Why, he thought. Why? Who removed them?

Underneath the sign, someone had added three more words in green paint:

DEAD CATS BOUNCE

Jack's stomach squirmed inside him. It looped the loop. Do they? Who wrote that?

Suddenly a blind shape reared up in front of Jack, right under his front wheel. He'd no choice but to ride straight over it, madly ringing his bell.

The shape yowled as it was tossed into the air, high over his head.

Jack, he didn't even look back to see whether it bounced.

The Vanishing Hitchhiker

The hitchhiker was standing a hundred yards or so from the roundabout. So that cars would see her before they picked up much speed, and be able to stop in the lay-by.

Graham did stop. He was a friendly man, and the hitchhiker looked much the same age as his own daughter.

'Seventeen,' she told him in her curious, fluting voice. She sat upright, rather still, rather quiet. And when Graham glanced at her in his rearview mirror, he thought she looked too pale for her own good. A bit sickly, he thought.

As Graham was driving into town, the girl asked him, 'Can you drop me off at this next turning? I live just down this road.'

Graham slowed right down and stopped. 'Hail Mary Road,' he said. 'That's a strange name.'

'Same as mine,' the girl told him. 'Mary. And I live at number seventeen. It all adds up.'

Then Mary thanked Graham and slid out of the car, and only when he got home did he see that she had left her raincoat lying on the back seat.

Silly girl! he thought. I know, I'll drop it off on my way home tomorrow.

When Graham rang the doorbell of number seventeen, a middle-aged woman opened the door.

'Hello!' said Graham, smiling. 'Mary's mother, I'll bet!' And then he held out the raincoat and explained how he'd given Mary a lift and she'd left the coat in the back of his car.

The woman smiled sadly. 'Yes,' she said. 'Yes.' She took the raincoat from Graham and hung it on a peg alongside several identical ones. 'She was killed in a crash at that roundabout, Mary was. Three years ago now. It would have been her birthday today.'

Fault Line

In the middle of the tunnel, the intercom crackled and then a voice, a woman's voice, announced: 'This train has developed a fault.'

The passengers tuned in. One groaned; one cupped his right ear; one raised her eyes.

More crackle, and then the same voice and the same announcement: 'This train has developed a fault.'

Everyone waited for the train to grind to a halt; everyone waited for an explanation. One couple laughed.

'Such as?' said one man.

'What is it this time?'

'The wrong kind of snow.'

'No,' said one man, 'we're going to be stuck in this tunnel, where we can't use our mobiles, until this time tomorrow.'

'We're going to Timbuktu.'

'Backwards.'

'We're going so far back we'll all end up before we were born.'

'No, it's not the train's fault. We've been boarded by cannibals.'

Still the train racketed on through the dark.

Crackle. Crackle.

And at last the woman's voice again. For real this time, not recorded.

'This train has developed a fault.'

'Tell us about it,' chorused several voices.

'No, it's not snowing and we're not going to be stuck in this tunnel and we're not on our way to Timbuktu and not going backwards to before we've been born. But yes, we *have* been boarded by cannibals.'

Several passengers immediately stood up and looked around them.

'Just joking,' said the woman on the intercom. 'This train has developed a fault. It keeps announcing it has developed a fault. This train has developed a fault.'

Mosquitoes

A man-eater. A blood-drunkard. That's what the giant was. His favourite meal was roasted human heart.

'He'll do for us all,' the people said.

'I'll stop him,' volunteered one young man, and he followed the giant's footprints along a dusty track. Then he lay down and pretended to be dead.

It wasn't long before the giant came stumping along the track. He found the young man and squashed his face with his hand.

'Still warm,' the giant growled. 'There's enough meat on him to feed my boy as well. People have grown so afraid of me they're dying of their own fear. I don't even have to kill them.'

The giant slung the young man over his back and carried him through the low entrance into his cavern. He threw him down beside his hearth—it jolted every bone in the young man's body—and then he went out to find some firewood.

At once the young man leaped up, and no sooner had he grabbed the giant's huge skinning-knife than the giant's boy strode in. He wasn't that much bigger than the young man, and in any case he was taken by surprise. The young man threw him and held the knife to his throat.

'Your father's heart,' he said. 'Where is it?'

'In his left heel,' the boy-giant told him.

Then the young man slit the boy-giant's throat, and dragged him to the back of the cavern.

Quite soon the giant came back, carrying an armful of firewood. As he ducked through the low entrance, the young man drove the knife into his left heel. The giant screamed in agony and fell on his face.

'Dead!' the young man shouted. 'Done for.'

'Dead, yes I'm dead,' the giant replied. 'But that won't stop me from eating you. You and everyone else in the world.'

'Never,' said the young man. 'You've eaten your last meal. You've drunk your last drop of blood.'

Then he lit the fire and cut the giant's body into joints and burned them.

The young man walked to the entrance of the cavern, and threw the giant's ashes to the whirling winds. A great cloud of ash.

Each particle of ash turned into a mosquito.

A cloud of mosquitoes swirled and skirled round the young man's head. They addled his brains. And out of the cloud he could hear a voice, taunting and whining.

'Yes, I'll eat you alive. You and everyone else in the world, until time ends.'

While he was listening, the young man was bitten by a mosquito. Then another. And another. They swarmed around him, they sucked his blood.

Why Everyone Needs to be Able to Tell a Story

It was cold and clammy, and I realized I'd never get back to our holiday cottage before dark.

But as I walked along the riverbank, I saw a light coming towards me. No, the mist was playing tricks. The light wasn't moving. I was. It was a little stone cottage.

'I'm lost,' I told the old man who opened the door. He had strange green eyes.

'I've only got one bed,' the old man said in a light, lilting voice. 'But I'll tell you what. You tell me a story, and you can sleep by the fire.'

Well, my head went empty. I couldn't think of a thing. You know how it is.

The old man's green eyes flickered. 'Pity,' he said. 'I could have done with a story. Still, you can stay if you want.' He waved towards the far corner of the room. 'Your companion won't be bothering you. Goodnight to you now.'

My companion. He was a sheep! Dead as a dumpster.

I sat down by the fire, and soon as I closed my eyes I heard the cottage door creak. Then I saw two men creep into the room, cross to the far corner, and pick up the dead sheep.

Well, I followed them. Of course I did. I didn't want the

poor old man thinking I'd rustled his dead sheep.

The two men hurried along the riverbank. Then one of them looked back over his shoulder.

'We're being followed!' he exclaimed.

'Come on!'

'Let's get him.'

At once the two men dropped the sheep—kerflup! They ran back towards me and me, I took off for the cottage. Fast as a hare.

You know what? I missed my footing, and tripped into the water. Right down. Right under, and back up.

In the misty dark, I caught hold of a slimy tree root, and the two thieves stood on the bank and shied stones at me. As if I was a coconut.

'Come on,' I heard one man say. 'We're wasting our time.'

And with that, they went back along the riverbank to the dead sheep.

I pulled on the root, but my feet slipped on the river mud.

I pulled again, but my hands slipped on the slimy root.

I pulled for a third time . . . and that's when I woke up.

Next morning, the first thing the old man said was: 'Well, I fancy you've a story now.'

'I have!' I exclaimed. 'I have. The moment I closed my eyes . . . '

The old man waved his right hand and his green eyes flickered. 'I know,' he said in his lilting voice. 'That dream! I gave it to you. Everyone needs to be able to tell a story.'

The Double-Tree

The two travellers were so thirsty and so hungry. They went from one house to another, but not a single villager unbolted a door or welcomed them with a warm word.

'The only one left is that tumbledown cottage up there on the mountainside,' one of them said.

It was a very poor place, thatched with reeds and rotting straw, but the kind old couple who lived there, Philemon and Baucis, greeted their guests warmly and ushered them in under the low lintel.

Baucis stirred the embers and threw wood on them, and before long the pot hanging over the fire began to bubble and sing.

Ah! Cabbage soup with little cubes of bacon. Curdled milk, and radishes to dip into it. Rosy apples. A wreath of purple grapes. A trickling honeycomb.

Philemon and Baucis gave the travellers as fine a meal as they were able. But then they saw that no matter how much more wine they poured out, their wine-bowl was still brimming, and they realized their guests were not men but gods. Jove and Mercury. They fell to their knees and begged forgiveness for such a simple meal.

Then Baucis went out and chased their precious goose, but the goose ran into the cottage, honking, and threw itself on the mercy of the gods.

'Don't harm her!' Jove said, smiling. 'And no harm will come to you, you kind, deserving couple. But the gods will punish the selfish people in the village below. Follow us now—up the mountainside.'

When they had almost reached the top, Philemon and Baucis turned round, and to their astonishment, they saw the whole village was drowned. Covered with a sheet of shining water. Only their own cottage stood high and dry, but it had changed into a temple with marble columns and a gleaming gold roof.

Philemon and Baucis wept for all their friends, their neighbours, but Jove and Mercury asked them, 'What is your greatest wish?'

The old couple conferred. 'To be keepers of your new temple,' Philemon replied. 'And since we've lived so long and happily together, allow us to die together.'

One day, when they were older than old, Philemon and Baucis were standing near the temple, telling worshippers how they had been visited by two gods, when each saw the other was coming into leaf. Branches, twigs, and leaves were sprouting from their bodies, covering their faces, rising over their heads.

Husband and wife, they went on talking to each other for as long as they could speak.

'Farewell,' they said. 'My dearest one! Farewell, my own.'

Outside the temple, the two trees grew with a double trunk. An oak with a lime-tree. A lime-tree with an oak. Their branches embraced.

Nightmare

'I didn't even know this room was up here,' I said. 'Not until I found it.'

'Right up under the roof,' said the boy. 'No fresh air. No light. This is where I'm locked in time. I just repeat myself.'

I shone my torch on him. He was my age, I think. But his skin was so pale—as if I were shining a light through a sheet or white flower or something. And his clothes were odd too. A big white collar. White cuffs.

'You'd look like me if you'd lived when I did,' said the boy.

'Can you come out?' I asked him.

'No,' said the boy. 'No, it's the opposite.'

'What do you mean?'

'I'm glad you've found me, anyhow,' said the boy. 'I've missed having someone to talk to. I died up here, you know. The lock sprang on me and I couldn't get out.'

'You're dead?'

Then I heard it. The lock, springing.

'I've never been properly buried,' said the boy. 'This is the repeating-room.'

From somewhere far away, I heard a hollow booming

86

sound. Somewhere below us. My father, calling my name.

'It's lunchtime,' I said.

'You can't go,' said the boy. 'There is no time up here. This is the repeating-room.'

'I didn't even know this room was up here,' I said. 'Not until I found it.'

'Right up under the roof,' the boy said. 'No fresh air. No light. This is where . . . '

I shone my torch on him. He was my age, I think.

Just One Gulp

Tanwen. That was her name. White fire.

And that's how she was with that wave of hair, ash blonde. And always playing with fire, always taking risks.

'You be careful,' her mother warned her. 'One day you'll go too far.'

One day Tanwen did go far, far up the mountainside behind her cottage, much further than she'd ever been before. She went without her brother, and climbed until she saw a little man sitting on a red-gold rock, drinking from his leather flask.

How thirsty she felt, flushed as she was, and husky.

'Thirsty?' asked the little man, and he held out the flask.

'Ta!' said Tanwen. 'Just one gulp, then.'

Oh! That juice. It tasted of . . . nectarine and blueberry and greengage, and every other kind of fruit ripened under the sun.

Tanwen smiled such a smile that it seemed to last for a year and a day, or even longer. Then she gave the leather flask back to the little man.

'Ta!' she said. 'I haven't seen you around before.'

'No,' said the little man.

Tanwen threw herself down on the ground and regained her breath. For a moment or two she closed her eyes. But then she said, 'I'd better be going down. My ma, she'll murder me.'

Down she went, Tanwen, skipping, slipping and slithering, down to the valley where she'd been born and always lived.

But as she came close to her village, Tanwen frowned. She screwed up her eyes and opened them again. The first cottage was no more than a wreck, a shell for the wind to sing in.

Tanwen ran her fingers through her ashen hair.

The second cottage was just like the first, and beyond that there was a brand new building, made of ugly breeze-blocks.

A woman was standing at the gate, cradling her baby. She stared at Tanwen. Her eyes bulged. They almost popped out of her head, and then she screamed.

'You!' she cried. 'You're that missing Tanwen!'

The woman held up her baby, she almost pushed her into Tanwen's face.

'The spitting image!' she cried. 'The spitting image of your . . . your great-niece. You're missing Tanwen!'

Tanwen, what did she see? What did she remember?

She gave a deep sigh, like a fire collapsing into itself. She sighed and dissolved into a pool of soft white ash.

My Story

When I walked out of the farmhouse I stepped straight into a story.

It was the blue hour and there were two monsters in Home Field. Each had five dazzling eyes. They were wearing scarlet armour, and roaring.

Our farm track passes between lots of oak trees, half-strangled by ivy, and as I neared them, someone loomed out of the gloom.

He was tall and thin, and wearing a strange sort of silver skull-cap, and over that a floppy dark hood. He wasn't walking towards me so much as loping, loping, uncoiling himself at each step.

I don't scare easily. 'Hi!' I called out as we passed each other.

Whoever he was, he didn't reply. He just kept walking with his head lowered, and I couldn't even see whether he had any eyes.

A few seconds later, I looked over my shoulder.

The man had stopped. He was looking over his shoulder too. He was watching me.

That's when I decided I'd better head back, even though it meant meeting him again.

The wind began to harrumph and growl, the old oaks groaned.

I squeezed my heavy torch. I'll cosh him with this, I thought. I will, if I have to.

Back in our warm kitchen, I asked my dad, 'Did you see him? Coming down the track?'

'Steady on, Freddie!' my dad said. 'Monsters . . . loping . . . silver skull-cap. You're imagining all this.'

'I am,' I said. 'I am. As soon as I went outside, I stepped straight into a story.'

Between Worlds

When the nurse walked down the hospital corridor with Zach's medicine, she was surprised to see him sitting up in bed. He was waving his arms and smiling and talking to some visitor who had pulled up his chair right beside him.

Poor Zach, she thought. He's only got a few weeks left, and I haven't seen him as happy as this for ages. I'll come back with his medicine later.

That's just what the nurse did, and at once Zach told her, 'It was my grandad.' His eyes were glowing. 'We talked about everything.'

The nurse ran into Zach's mother when she came to see him late that afternoon. 'You're not his first visitor today,' she said. 'His grandad was here just an hour ago, and Zach was ever so pleased to see him.'

Zach's mother shook her head. 'He hasn't got a grandad,' she replied.

'But . . . ' the nurse began.

'No,' said Zach's mother, 'my husband never knew his own father, and mine died three years ago.'

'Really?' exclaimed the nurse. 'He told Zach about how

afraid of the dark you were as a girl, and how there's nothing to fear.'

Zach's mother shivered, she hugged herself.

'Yes,' the nurse said. 'He was sitting right beside the bed. I saw him with my own eyes.'

Storybirds

He was ancient. He'd run out of puff. Out of time, almost. And he knew the day had come to give his old stories to new storytellers.

In the cobbled market-place, under the dusty plane tree with all its outstretched hands, dozens of children plumped themselves down on the ground, and their parents and grandparents and great-grandparents planted themselves on café chairs.

'There was a tree,' began the storyteller. 'This tree here, actually. Very old. Ancient. But it was alive with birds. Hundreds. Thousands of them. Every colour under the sun. Singing all the secrets and half-hopes and joys and fears and grief of this world of ours.

'Then,' the old man told them, 'one bird flew away.'

He pursed his lips and rippled his tongue behind the broken bars of his teeth.

'Th-rrrrr!'

The storyteller looked round at all the children and parents and grandparents and great-grandparents sitting in the market-place.

'What then?' a boy called out.

The old man's lips twitched. He parted them a little.

'Th-rrrr!' Again he rippled his tongue behind his teeth, a little lighter and higher than before.

'What then?' a girl called out.

'Th-rrrr!'

'Then?'

'Th-rrrr!'

'Go on, then!'

'Th-rrrr!'

One man waved his hands. 'How long's this going to go on for?'

The old storyteller looked up at the plane tree and half-closed his eyes. 'Oh!' he said, and he yawned. 'Until all the birds have gone.'

Acknowledgements

Some of these stories are original. Others retell or are more loosely based on traditional tales I have found in *The Vanishing Hitchhiker* by Jan Harold Brunvand (New York, 1981) and *Too Good to be True* by Jan Harold Brunvand (New York, 1999); *American Indian Myths and Legends,* selected and edited by Richard Erdoes and Alfonso Ortiz (New York, 1984); *Kinder- und Hausmärchen* by Jacob and Wilhelm Grimm (1812); *Memorials of a Quiet Life* by Augustus Hare (1871); Ovid's *Metamorphoses*; *Folktales from India* by A. K. Ramanujan (New York, 1991); *Japanese Tales,* edited and translated by Royall Tyler (New York, 1987); *Folk Tales from Russian Lands* (New York, 1963) first published under the title *A Mountain of Gems: Fairy-Tales of the Peoples of the Soviet Land* (Moscow, 1963).

'Dathera Dad' was first published in my *British Folk Tales* (London, 1987). And my youngest daughter, Eleanor, and I co-authored the book's shortest story!

Liz Cross and the Oxford University Press have shown monumental patience in their long wait for this little book, and Clare Whitston has skilfully edited it. I'm most grateful to Joe Edwardes-Evans for his advice on grind-bars and the like, Twiggy Bigwood for typing and retyping many a draft, and above all my eagle-eyed wife Linda for whom short has never been quite short enough.